Preface to Major
First Aid to C

Bernard Shaw

Alpha Editions

This edition published in 2024

ISBN 9789361474606

Design and Setting By

Alpha Editions

www.alphaedis.com

Email - info@alphaedis.com

Contents

BERNARD SHAW

N.B. The Euripidean verses in the second act of Major Barbara are not by me, or even directly by Euripides. They are by Professor Gilbert Murray, whose English version of The Baccha; came into our dramatic literature with all the impulsive power of an original work shortly before Major Barbara was begun. The play, indeed, stands indebted to him in more ways than one.

G. B. S.

Before dealing with the deeper aspects of Major Barbara, let me, for the credit of English literature, make a protest against an unpatriotic habit into which many of my critics have fallen. Whenever my view strikes them as being at all outside the range of, say, an ordinary suburban churchwarden, they conclude that I am echoing Schopenhauer, Nietzsche, Ibsen, Strindberg, Tolstoy, or some other heresiarch in northern or eastern Europe.

I confess there is something flattering in this simple faith in my accomplishment as a linguist and my erudition as a philosopher. But I cannot tolerate the assumption that life and literature is so poor in these islands that we must go abroad for all dramatic material that is not common and all ideas that are not superficial. I therefore venture to put my critics in possession of certain facts concerning my contact with modern ideas.

About half a century ago, an Irish novelist, Charles Lever, wrote a story entitled A Day's Ride: A Life's Romance. It was published by Charles Dickens in Household Words, and proved so strange to the public taste that Dickens pressed Lever to make short work of it. I read scraps of this novel when I was a child; and it made an enduring impression on me. The hero was a very romantic hero, trying to live bravely, chivalrously, and powerfully by dint of mere romance-fed imagination, without courage, without means, without knowledge, without skill, without anything real except his bodily appetites. Even in my childhood I found in this poor devil's unsuccessful encounters with the facts of life, a poignant quality that romantic fiction lacked. The book, in spite of its first failure, is not dead: I saw its title the other day in the catalogue of Tauchnitz.

Now why is it that when I also deal in the tragi-comic irony of the conflict between real life and the romantic imagination, no critic ever affiliates me to my countryman and immediate forerunner, Charles Lever, whilst they confidently derive me from a Norwegian author of whose language I do not know three words, and of whom I knew nothing until years after the Shavian Anschauung was already unequivocally declared in books full of what came, ten years later, to be perfunctorily labelled Ibsenism. I was not Ibsenist even at second hand; for Lever, though he may have read Henri Beyle, alias Stendhal, certainly never read Ibsen. Of the books that made Lever popular, such as Charles O'Malley and Harry Lorrequer, I know nothing but the names and some of the illustrations. But the story of the day's ride and life's romance of Potts (claiming alliance with Pozzo di Borgo) caught me and fascinated me as something strange and significant, though I already knew all about Alnaschar and Don Quixote and Simon Tappertit and many another romantic hero mocked by reality. From the plays of Aristophanes to the tales of Stevenson that mockery has been made familiar to all who are properly saturated with letters.

Where, then, was the novelty in Lever's tale? Partly, I think, in a new seriousness in dealing with Potts's disease. Formerly, the contrast between madness and sanity was deemed comic: Hogarth shows us how fashionable people went in parties to Bedlam to laugh at the lunatics. I myself have had a village idiot exhibited to me as some thing irresistibly funny. On the stage the madman was once a regular comic figure; that was how Hamlet got his opportunity before Shakespear touched him. The originality of Shakespear's version lay in his taking the lunatic sympathetically and seriously, and thereby making an advance towards the eastern consciousness of the fact that lunacy may be inspiration in disguise, since a man who has more brains than his fellows necessarily appears as mad to them as one who has less. But Shakespear did not do for Pistol and Parolles what he did for Hamlet. The particular sort of madman they represented, the romantic makebeliever, lay outside the pale of sympathy in literature: he was pitilessly despised and ridiculed here as he was in the east under the name of Alnaschar, and was doomed to be, centuries later, under the name of Simon Tappertit. When Cervantes relented over Don Quixote, and Dickens relented over Pickwick, they did not become impartial: they simply changed sides, and became friends and apologists where they had formerly been mockers.

In Lever's story there is a real change of attitude. There is no relenting towards Potts: he never gains our affections like Don Quixote and Pickwick: he has not even the infatuate courage of Tappertit. But we dare not laugh at him, because, somehow, we recognize ourselves in Potts. We may, some of us, have enough nerve, enough muscle, enough luck, enough tact or skill or address or knowledge to carry things off better than he did; to impose on the people who saw through him; to fascinate Katinka (who cut Potts so ruthlessly at the end of the story); but for all that, we know that Potts plays an enormous part in ourselves and in the world, and that the social problem is not a problem of story-book heroes of the older pattern, but a problem of Pottses, and of how to make men of them. To fall back on my old phrase, we have the feeling—one that Alnaschar, Pistol, Parolles, and Tappertit never gave us—that Potts is a piece of really scientific natural history as distinguished from comic story telling. His author is not throwing a stone at a creature of another and inferior order, but making a confession, with the effect that the stone hits everybody full in the conscience and causes their self-esteem to smart very sorely. Hence the failure of Lever's book to please the readers of Household Words. That pain in the self-esteem nowadays causes critics to raise a cry of Ibsenism. I therefore assure them that the sensation first came to me from Lever and may have come to him from Beyle, or at least out of the Stendhalian atmosphere. I exclude the hypothesis of complete originality on Lever's part, because a man can no more be completely original in that sense than a tree can grow out of air.

Another mistake as to my literary ancestry is made whenever I violate the romantic convention that all women are angels when they are not devils; that they are better looking than men; that their part in courtship is entirely passive; and that the human female form is the most beautiful object in nature. Schopenhauer wrote a splenetic essay which, as it is neither polite nor profound, was probably intended to knock this nonsense violently on the head. A sentence denouncing the idolized form as ugly has been largely quoted. The English critics have read that sentence; and I must here affirm, with as much gentleness as the implication will bear, that it has yet to be proved that they have dipped any deeper. At all events, whenever an English playwright represents a young and marriageable woman as being anything but a romantic heroine, he is disposed of without further thought as an echo of Schopenhauer. My own case is a specially hard one, because, when I implore the critics who are obsessed with the Schopenhaurian formula to remember that playwrights, like sculptors, study their figures from life, and not from philosophic essays, they reply passionately that I am not a playwright and that my stage figures do not live. But even so, I may and do ask them why, if they must give the credit of my plays to a philosopher, they do not give it to an English philosopher? Long before I ever read a word by Schopenhauer, or even knew whether he was a philosopher or a chemist, the Socialist revival of the eighteen-eighties brought me into contact, both literary and personal, with Mr Ernest Belfort Bax, an English Socialist and philosophic essayist, whose handling of modern feminism would provoke romantic protests from Schopenhauer himself, or even Strindberg. As a matter of fact I hardly noticed Schopenhauer's disparagements of women when they came under my notice later on, so thoroughly had Mr Bax familiarized me with the homoist attitude, and forced me to recognize the extent to which public opinion, and consequently legislation and jurisprudence, is corrupted by feminist sentiment.

But Mr Bax's essays were not confined to the Feminist question. He was a ruthless critic of current morality. Other writers have gained sympathy for dramatic criminals by eliciting the alleged "soul of goodness in things evil"; but Mr Bax would propound some quite undramatic and apparently shabby violation of our commercial law and morality, and not merely defend it with the most disconcerting ingenuity, but actually prove it to be a positive duty that nothing but the certainty of police persecution should prevent every right-minded man from at once doing on principle. The Socialists were naturally shocked, being for the most part morbidly moral people; but at all events they were saved later on from the delusion that nobody but Nietzsche had ever challenged our mercanto-Christian morality. I first heard the name of Nietzsche from a German mathematician, Miss Borchardt, who had read my Quintessence of Ibsenism, and told me that she saw what I had been reading: namely, Nietzsche's Jenseits von Gut and Bose. Which I protest I had never seen, and could not have read with any comfort, for want of the necessary German, if I had seen it.

Nietzsche, like Schopenhauer, is the victim in England of a single much quoted sentence containing the phrase "big blonde beast." On the strength of this alliteration it is assumed that Nietzsche gained his European reputation by a senseless glorification of selfish bullying as the rule of life, just as it is assumed, on the strength of the single word Superman (Ubermensch) borrowed by me from Nietzsche, that I look for the salvation of society to the despotism of a single Napoleonic Superman, in spite of my careful demonstration of the folly of that outworn infatuation. But even the less recklessly superficial critics seem to believe that the modern objection to Christianity as a pernicious slave-morality was first put forward by Nietzsche. It was familiar to me before I ever heard of Nietzsche. The late Captain Wilson, author of several queer pamphlets, propagandist of a metaphysical system called Comprehensionism, and inventor of the term "Crosstianity" to distinguish the retrograde element in Christendom, was wont thirty years ago, in the discussions of the Dialectical Society, to protest earnestly against the beatitudes of the Sermon on the Mount as excuses for cowardice and servility, as destructive of our will, and consequently of our honor and manhood. Now it is true that Captain Wilson's moral criticism of Christianity was not a historical theory of it, like Nietzsche's; but this objection cannot be made to Mr Stuart-Glennie, the successor of Buckle as a philosophic historian, who has devoted his life to the elaboration and propagation of his theory that Christianity is part of an epoch (or rather an aberration, since it began as recently as 6000BC and is already collapsing) produced by the necessity in which the numerically inferior white races found themselves to impose their domination on the colored races by priestcraft, making a virtue and a popular religion of drudgery and submissiveness in this world not only as a means of achieving saintliness of character but of securing a reward in heaven. Here you have the slave-morality view formulated by a Scotch philosopher long before English writers began chattering about Nietzsche.

As Mr Stuart-Glennie traced the evolution of society to the conflict of races, his theory made some sensation among Socialists—that is, among the only people who were seriously thinking about historical evolution at all—by its collision with the class-conflict theory of Karl Marx. Nietzsche, as I gather, regarded the slave-morality as having been invented and imposed on the world by slaves making a virtue of necessity and a religion of their servitude. Mr Stuart-Glennie regards the slave-morality as an invention of the superior white race to subjugate the minds of the inferior races whom they wished to exploit, and who would have destroyed them by force of numbers if their minds had not been subjugated. As this process is in operation still, and can be studied at first hand not only in our Church schools and in the struggle between our modern proprietary classes and the proletariat, but in the part played by Christian missionaries in reconciling the black races of Africa to their subjugation by European Capitalism, we can judge for ourselves whether the initiative came from above or below. My object here is not to argue the historical point, but simply to make our theatre critics ashamed of their habit of treating Britain as an intellectual void, and assuming that every philosophical idea, every historic theory, every criticism of our moral, religious and juridical institutions, must necessarily be either imported from abroad, or else a fantastic sally (in rather questionable taste) totally unrelated to the existing body of thought. I urge them to remember that this body of thought is the slowest of growths and the rarest of blossomings, and that if there is such a thing on the philosophic plane as a matter of course, it is that no individual can make more than a minute contribution to it. In fact, their conception of clever persons parthenogenetically bringing forth complete original cosmogonies by dint of sheer "brilliancy" is part of that ignorant credulity which is the despair of the honest philosopher, and the opportunity of the religious impostor.

THE GOSPEL OF ST. ANDREW UNDERSHAFT

It is this credulity that drives me to help my critics out with Major Barbara by telling them what to say about it. In the millionaire Undershaft I have represented a man who has become intellectually and spiritually as well as practically conscious of the irresistible natural truth which we all abhor and repudiate: to wit, that the greatest of evils and the worst of crimes is poverty, and that our first duty—a duty to which every other consideration should be sacrificed—is not to be poor. "Poor but honest," "the respectable poor," and such phrases are as intolerable and as immoral as "drunken but amiable," "fraudulent but a good after-dinner speaker," "splendidly criminal," or the like. Security, the chief pretence of civilization, cannot exist where the worst of dangers, the danger of poverty, hangs over everyone's head, and where the alleged protection of our persons from violence is only an accidental result of the existence of a police force whose real business is to force the poor man to see his children starve whilst idle people overfeed pet dogs with the money that might feed and clothe them.

It is exceedingly difficult to make people realize that an evil is an evil. For instance, we seize a man and deliberately do him a malicious injury: say, imprison him for years. One would not suppose that it needed any exceptional clearness of wit to recognize in this an act of diabolical cruelty. But in England such a recognition provokes a stare of surprise, followed by an explanation that the outrage is punishment or justice or something else that is all right, or perhaps by a heated attempt to argue that we should all be robbed and murdered in our beds if such senseless villainies as sentences of imprisonment were not committed daily. It is useless to argue that even if this were true, which it is not, the alternative to adding crimes of our own to the crimes from which we suffer is not helpless submission. Chickenpox is an evil; but if I were to declare that we must either submit to it or else repress it sternly by seizing everyone who suffers from it and punishing them by inoculation with smallpox, I should be laughed at; for though nobody could deny that the result would be to prevent chickenpox to some extent by making people avoid it much more carefully, and to effect a further apparent prevention by making them conceal it very anxiously, yet people would have sense enough to see that the deliberate propagation of smallpox was a creation of evil, and must therefore be ruled out in favor of purely humane and hygienic measures. Yet in the precisely parallel case of a man breaking into my house and stealing my wife's diamonds I am expected as a matter of course to steal ten years of his life, torturing him all the time. If he tries to defeat that monstrous retaliation by shooting me, my survivors hang him. The net result suggested by the police statistics is that we inflict atrocious injuries on the burglars we catch in order to make the rest take effectual precautions against detection; so that instead of saving our wives' diamonds from burglary we only greatly decrease our chances of ever getting them back, and increase our chances of being shot by the robber if we are unlucky enough to disturb him at his work.

But the thoughtless wickedness with which we scatter sentences of imprisonment, torture in the solitary cell and on the plank bed, and flogging, on moral invalids and energetic rebels, is as nothing compared to the stupid levity with which we tolerate poverty as if it were either a wholesome tonic for lazy people or else a virtue to be embraced as St Francis embraced it. If a man is indolent, let him be poor. If he is drunken, let him be poor. If he is not a gentleman, let him be poor. If he is addicted to the fine arts or to pure science instead of to trade and finance, let him be poor. If he chooses to spend his urban eighteen shillings a week or his agricultural thirteen shillings a week on his beer and his family instead of saving it up for his old age, let him be poor. Let nothing be done for "the undeserving": let him be poor. Serve him right! Also—somewhat inconsistently—blessed are the poor!

Now what does this Let Him Be Poor mean? It means let him be weak. Let him be ignorant. Let him become a nucleus of disease. Let him be a standing exhibition and example of ugliness and dirt. Let him have rickety children. Let him be cheap and let him drag his fellows down to his price by selling himself to do their work. Let his habitations turn our cities into poisonous congeries of slums. Let his daughters infect our young men with the diseases of the streets and his sons revenge him by turning the nation's manhood into scrofula, cowardice, cruelty, hypocrisy, political imbecility, and all the other fruits of oppression and malnutrition. Let the undeserving become still less deserving; and let the deserving lay up for himself, not treasures in heaven, but horrors in hell upon earth. This being so, is it really wise to let him be poor? Would he not do ten times less harm as a prosperous burglar, incendiary, ravisher or murderer, to the utmost limits of humanity's comparatively negligible impulses in these directions? Suppose we were to abolish all penalties for such activities, and decide that poverty is the one thing we will not tolerate—that every adult with less than, say, 365 pounds a year, shall be painlessly but inexorably killed, and every hungry half naked child forcibly fattened and clothed, would not that be an enormous improvement on our existing system, which has already destroyed so many civilizations, and is visibly destroying ours in the same way?

Is there any radicle of such legislation in our parliamentary system? Well, there are two measures just sprouting in the political soil, which may conceivably grow to something valuable. One is the institution of a Legal Minimum Wage. The other, Old Age Pensions. But there is a better plan than either of these. Some time ago I mentioned the subject of Universal Old Age Pensions to my fellow Socialist Mr Cobden-Sanderson, famous as an artist-craftsman in bookbinding and printing. "Why not Universal Pensions for Life?" said Cobden-Sanderson. In saying this, he solved the industrial problem at a stroke. At present we say callously to each citizen: "If you want money, earn it," as if his having or not having it were a matter that concerned himself alone. We do not even secure for him the opportunity of earning it: on the contrary, we allow our industry to be organized in open dependence on the maintenance of "a reserve army of unemployed" for the sake of "elasticity." The sensible course would be Cobden-Sanderson's: that is, to give every man enough to live well on, so as to guarantee the community against the possibility of a case of the malignant disease of poverty, and then (necessarily) to see that he earned it.

Undershaft, the hero of Major Barbara, is simply a man who, having grasped the fact that poverty is a crime, knows that when society offered him the alternative of poverty or a lucrative trade in death and destruction, it offered him, not a choice between opulent villainy and humble virtue, but between energetic enterprise and cowardly infamy. His conduct stands the Kantian test, which Peter Shirley's does not. Peter Shirley is what we call the honest poor man. Undershaft is what we call the wicked rich one: Shirley is Lazarus, Undershaft Dives. Well, the misery of the world is due to the fact that the great mass of men act and believe as Peter Shirley acts and believes. If they acted and believed as Undershaft acts and believes, the immediate result would be a revolution of incalculable beneficence. To be wealthy, says Undershaft, is with me a point of honor for which I am prepared to kill at the risk of my own life. This preparedness is, as he says, the final test of sincerity. Like Froissart's medieval hero, who saw that "to rob and pill was a good life," he is not the dupe of that public sentiment against killing which is propagated and endowed by people who would otherwise be killed themselves, or of the mouth-honor paid to poverty and obedience by rich and insubordinate do-nothings who want to rob the poor without courage and command them without superiority. Froissart's knight, in placing the achievement of a good life before all the other duties—which indeed are not duties at all when they conflict with it, but plain wickednesses—behaved bravely, admirably, and, in the final analysis, public-spiritedly. Medieval society, on the other hand, behaved very badly indeed in organizing itself so stupidly that a good life could be achieved by robbing and pilling. If the knight's contemporaries had been all as resolute as he, robbing and pilling would have been the shortest way to the gallows, just as, if we were all as resolute and clearsighted as Undershaft, an attempt to live by means of what is called "an independent income" would be the shortest way to the lethal chamber. But as, thanks to our political imbecility and personal cowardice (fruits of poverty both), the best imitation of a good life now procurable is life on an independent income, all sensible people aim at securing such an income, and are, of course, careful to legalize and moralize both it and all the actions and sentiments which lead to it and support it as an institution. What else can they do? They know, of course, that they are rich because others are poor. But they cannot help that: it is for the poor to repudiate poverty when they have had enough of it. The thing can be done easily enough: the demonstrations to the contrary made by the economists, jurists, moralists and sentimentalists hired by the rich to defend them, or even doing the work gratuitously out of sheer folly and abjectness, impose only on the hirers.

The reason why the independent income-tax payers are not solid in defence of their position is that since we are not medieval rovers through a sparsely populated country, the poverty of those we rob prevents our having the good life for which we sacrifice them. Rich men or aristocrats with a developed sense of life—men like Ruskin and William Morris and Kropotkin—have enormous social appetites and very fastidious personal ones. They are not content with handsome houses: they want handsome cities. They are not content with bediamonded wives and blooming daughters: they complain because the charwoman is badly dressed, because the laundress smells of gin, because the sempstress is anemic, because every man they meet is not a friend and every woman not a romance. They turn up their noses at their neighbors' drains, and are made ill by the architecture of their neighbors' houses. Trade patterns made to suit vulgar people do not please them (and they can get nothing else): they cannot sleep nor sit at ease upon "slaughtered" cabinet makers' furniture. The very air is not good enough for them: there is too much factory smoke in it. They even demand abstract conditions: justice, honor, a noble moral atmosphere, a mystic nexus to replace the cash nexus. Finally they declare that though to rob and pill with your own hand on horseback and in steel coat may have been a good life, to rob and pill by the hands of the policeman, the bailiff, and the soldier, and to underpay them meanly for doing it, is not a good life, but rather fatal to all possibility of even a tolerable one. They call on the poor to revolt, and, finding the poor shocked at their ungentlemanliness, despairingly revile the proletariat for its "damned wantlessness" (verdammte Bedurfnislosigkeit).

So far, however, their attack on society has lacked simplicity. The poor do not share their tastes nor understand their art-criticisms. They do not want the simple life, nor the esthetic life; on the contrary, they want very much to wallow in all the costly vulgarities from which the elect souls among the rich turn away with loathing. It is by surfeit and not by abstinence that they will be cured of their hankering after unwholesome sweets. What they do dislike and despise and are ashamed of is poverty. To ask them to fight for the difference between the Christmas number of the Illustrated London News and the Kelmscott Chaucer is silly: they prefer the News. The difference between a stockbroker's cheap and dirty starched white shirt and collar and the comparatively costly and carefully dyed blue shirt of William Morris is a difference so disgraceful to Morris in their eyes that if they fought on the subject at all, they would fight in defence of the starch. "Cease to be slaves, in order that you may become cranks" is not a very inspiring call to arms; nor is it really improved by substituting saints for cranks. Both terms denote men of genius; and the common man does not want to live the life of a man of genius: he would much rather live the life of a pet collie if that were the only alternative. But he does want more money. Whatever else he may be vague about, he is clear about that. He may or may not prefer Major Barbara to the Drury Lane pantomime; but he always prefers five hundred pounds to five hundred shillings.

Now to deplore this preference as sordid, and teach children that it is sinful to desire money, is to strain towards the extreme possible limit of impudence in lying, and corruption in hypocrisy. The universal regard for money is the one hopeful fact in our civilization, the one sound spot in our social conscience. Money is the most important thing in the world. It represents health, strength, honor, generosity and beauty as conspicuously and undeniably as the want of it represents illness, weakness, disgrace, meanness and ugliness. Not the least of its virtues is that it destroys base people as certainly as it fortifies and dignifies noble people. It is only when it is cheapened to worthlessness for some, and made impossibly dear to others, that it becomes a curse. In short, it is a curse only in such foolish social conditions that life itself is a curse. For the two things are inseparable: money is the counter that enables life to be distributed socially: it is life as truly as sovereigns and bank notes are money. The first duty of every citizen is to insist on having money on reasonable terms; and this demand is not complied with by giving four men three shillings each for ten or twelve hours' drudgery and one man a thousand pounds for nothing. The crying need of the nation is not for better morals, cheaper bread, temperance, liberty, culture, redemption of fallen sisters and erring brothers, nor the grace, love and fellowship of the Trinity, but simply for enough money. And the evil to be attacked is not sin, suffering, greed, priestcraft, kingcraft, demagogy, monopoly, ignorance, drink, war, pestilence, nor any other of the scapegoats which reformers sacrifice, but simply poverty.

Once take your eyes from the ends of the earth and fix them on this truth just under your nose; and Andrew Undershaft's views will not perplex you in the least. Unless indeed his constant sense that he is only the instrument of a Will or Life Force which uses him for purposes wider than his own, may puzzle you. If so, that is because you are walking either in artificial Darwinian darkness, or to mere stupidity. All genuinely religious people have that consciousness. To them Undershaft the Mystic will be quite intelligible, and his perfect comprehension of his daughter the Salvationist and her lover the Euripidean republican natural and inevitable. That, however, is not new, even on the stage. What is new, as far as I know, is that article in Undershaft's religion which recognizes in Money the first need and in poverty the vilest sin of man and society.

This dramatic conception has not, of course, been attained per saltum. Nor has it been borrowed from Nietzsche or from any man born beyond the Channel. The late Samuel Butler, in his own department the greatest English writer of the latter half of the XIX century, steadily inculcated the necessity and morality of a conscientious Laodiceanism in religion and of an earnest and constant sense of the importance of money. It drives one almost to despair of English literature when one sees so extraordinary a study of English life as Butler's posthumous Way of All Flesh making so little impression that when, some years later, I produce plays in which Butler's extraordinarily fresh, free and future-piercing suggestions have an obvious share, I am met with nothing but vague cacklings about Ibsen and Nietzsche, and am only too thankful that they are not about Alfred de Musset and Georges Sand. Really, the English do not deserve to have great men. They allowed Butler to die practically unknown, whilst I, a comparatively insignificant Irish journalist, was leading them by the nose into an advertisement of me which has made my own life a burden. In Sicily there is a Via Samuele Butler. When an English tourist sees it, he either asks "Who the devil was Samuele Butler?" or wonders why the Sicilians should perpetuate the memory of the author of Hudibras.

Well, it cannot be denied that the English are only too anxious to recognize a man of genius if somebody will kindly point him out to them. Having pointed myself out in this manner with some success, I now point out Samuel Butler, and trust that in consequence I shall hear a little less in future of the novelty and foreign origin of the ideas which are now making their way into the English theatre through plays written by Socialists. There are living men whose originality and power are as obvious as Butler's; and when they die that fact will be discovered. Meanwhile I recommend them to insist on their own merits as an important part of their own business.

THE SALVATION ARMY

When Major Barbara was produced in London, the second act was reported in an important northern newspaper as a withering attack on the Salvation Army, and the despairing ejaculation of Barbara deplored by a London daily as a tasteless blasphemy. And they were set right, not by the professed critics of the theatre, but by religious and philosophical publicists like Sir Oliver Lodge and Dr Stanton Coit, and strenuous Nonconformist journalists like Mr William Stead, who not only understood the act as well as the Salvationists themselves, but also saw it in its relation to the religious life of the nation, a life which seems to lie not only outside the sympathy of many of our theatre critics, but actually outside their knowledge of society. Indeed nothing could be more ironically curious than the confrontation Major Barbara effected of the theatre enthusiasts with the religious enthusiasts. On the one hand was the playgoer, always seeking pleasure, paying exorbitantly for it, suffering unbearable discomforts for it, and hardly ever getting it. On the other hand was the Salvationist, repudiating gaiety and courting effort and sacrifice, yet always in the wildest spirits, laughing, joking, singing, rejoicing, drumming, and tambourining: his life flying by in a flash of excitement, and his death arriving as a climax of triumph. And, if you please, the playgoer despising the Salvationist as a joyless person, shut out from the heaven of the theatre, self-condemned to a life of hideous gloom; and the Salvationist mourning over the playgoer as over a prodigal with vine leaves in his hair, careering outrageously to hell amid the popping of champagne corks and the ribald laughter of sirens! Could misunderstanding be more complete, or sympathy worse misplaced?

Fortunately, the Salvationists are more accessible to the religious character of the drama than the playgoers to the gay energy and artistic fertility of religion. They can see, when it is pointed out to them, that a theatre, as a place where two or three are gathered together, takes from that divine presence an inalienable sanctity of which the grossest and profanest farce can no more deprive it than a hypocritical sermon by a snobbish bishop can desecrate Westminster Abbey. But in our professional playgoers this indispensable preliminary conception of sanctity seems wanting. They talk of actors as mimes and mummers, and, I fear, think of dramatic authors as liars and pandars, whose main business is the voluptuous soothing of the tired city speculator when what he calls the serious business of the day is over. Passion, the life of drama, means nothing to them but primitive sexual excitement: such phrases as "impassioned poetry" or "passionate love of truth" have fallen quite out of their vocabulary and been replaced by "passional crime" and the like. They assume, as far as I can gather, that people in whom passion has a larger scope are passionless and therefore uninteresting. Consequently they come to think of religious people as people who are not interesting and not amusing. And so, when Barbara cuts the regular Salvation Army jokes, and snatches a kiss from her lover across his drum, the devotees of the theatre think they ought to appear shocked, and conclude that the whole play is an elaborate mockery of the Army. And then either hypocritically rebuke me for mocking, or foolishly take part in the supposed mockery! Even the handful of mentally competent critics got into difficulties over my demonstration of the economic deadlock in which the Salvation Army finds itself. Some of them thought that the Army would not have taken money from a distiller and a cannon founder: others thought it should not have taken it: all assumed more or less definitely that it reduced itself to absurdity or hypocrisy by taking it. On the first point the reply of the Army itself was prompt and conclusive. As one of its officers said, they would take money from the devil himself and be only too glad to get it out of his hands and into God's. They gratefully acknowledged that publicans not only give them money but allow them to collect it in the bar—sometimes even when there is a Salvation meeting outside preaching teetotalism. In fact, they questioned the verisimilitude of the play, not because Mrs Baines took the money, but because Barbara refused it.

On the point that the Army ought not to take such money, its justification is obvious. It must take the money because it cannot exist without money, and there is no other money to be had. Practically all the spare money in the country consists of a mass of rent, interest, and profit, every penny of which is bound up with crime, drink, prostitution, disease, and all the evil fruits of poverty, as inextricably as with enterprise, wealth, commercial probity, and national prosperity. The notion that you can earmark certain coins as tainted is an unpractical individualist superstition. None the less the fact that all our money is tainted gives a very severe shock to earnest young souls when some dramatic instance of the taint first makes them conscious of it. When an enthusiastic young clergyman of the Established Church first realizes that the Ecclesiastical Commissioners receive the rents of sporting public houses, brothels, and sweating dens; or that the most generous contributor at his last charity sermon was an employer trading in female labor cheapened by prostitution as unscrupulously as a hotel keeper trades in waiters' labor cheapened by tips, or commissionaire's labor cheapened by pensions; or that the only patron who can afford to rebuild his church or his schools or give his boys' brigade a gymnasium or a library is the son-in-law of a Chicago meat King, that young clergyman has, like Barbara, a very bad quarter hour. But he cannot help himself by refusing to accept money from anybody except sweet old ladies with independent incomes and gentle and lovely ways of life. He has only to follow up the income of the sweet ladies to its industrial source, and there he will find Mrs Warren's profession and the poisonous canned meat and all the rest of it. His own stipend has the same root. He must either share the world's guilt or go to another planet. He must save the world's honor if he is to save his own. This is what all the Churches find just as the Salvation Army and Barbara find it in the play. Her discovery that she is her father's accomplice; that the Salvation Army is the accomplice of the distiller and the dynamite maker; that they can no more escape one another than they can escape the air they breathe; that there is no salvation for them through personal righteousness, but only through the redemption of the whole nation from its vicious, lazy, competitive anarchy: this discovery has been made by everyone except the Pharisees and (apparently) the professional playgoers, who still wear their Tom Hood shirts and underpay their washerwomen without the slightest misgiving as to the elevation of their private characters, the purity of their private atmospheres, and their right to repudiate as foreign to themselves the coarse depravity of the garret and the slum. Not that they mean any harm: they only desire to be, in their little private way, what they call gentlemen. They do not understand Barbara's lesson because they have not, like her, learnt it by taking their part in the larger life of the nation.

BARBARA'S RETURN TO THE COLORS.

Barbara's return to the colors may yet provide a subject for the dramatic historian of the future. To go back to the Salvation Army with the knowledge that even the Salvationists themselves are not saved yet; that poverty is not blessed, but a most damnable sin; and that when General Booth chose Blood and Fire for the emblem of Salvation instead of the Cross, he was perhaps better inspired than he knew: such knowledge, for the daughter of Andrew Undershaft, will clearly lead to something hopefuller than distributing bread and treacle at the expense of Bodger.

It is a very significant thing, this instinctive choice of the military form of organization, this substitution of the drum for the organ, by the Salvation Army. Does it not suggest that the Salvationists divine that they must actually fight the devil instead of merely praying at him? At present, it is true, they have not quite ascertained his correct address. When they do, they may give a very rude shock to that sense of security which he has gained from his experience of the fact that hard words, even when uttered by eloquent essayists and lecturers, or carried unanimously at enthusiastic public meetings on the motion of eminent reformers, break no bones. It has been said that the French Revolution was the work of Voltaire, Rousseau and the Encyclopedists. It seems to me to have been the work of men who had observed that virtuous indignation, caustic criticism, conclusive argument and instructive pamphleteering, even when done by the most earnest and witty literary geniuses, were as useless as praying, things going steadily from bad to worse whilst the Social Contract and the pamphlets of Voltaire were at the height of their vogue. Eventually, as we know, perfectly respectable citizens and earnest philanthropists connived at the September massacres because hard experience had convinced them that if they contented themselves with appeals to humanity and patriotism, the aristocracy, though it would read their appeals with the greatest enjoyment and appreciation, flattering and admiring the writers, would none the less continue to conspire with foreign monarchists to undo the revolution and restore the old system with every circumstance of savage vengeance and ruthless repression of popular liberties.

The nineteenth century saw the same lesson repeated in England. It had its Utilitarians, its Christian Socialists, its Fabians (still extant): it had Bentham, Mill, Dickens, Ruskin, Carlyle, Butler, Henry George, and Morris. And the end of all their efforts is the Chicago described by Mr Upton Sinclair, and the London in which the people who pay to be amused by my dramatic representation of Peter Shirley turned out to starve at forty because there are younger slaves to be had for his wages, do not take, and have not the slightest intention of taking, any effective step to organize society in such a way as to make that everyday infamy impossible. I, who have preached and pamphleteered like any Encyclopedist, have to confess that my methods are no use, and would be no use if I were Voltaire, Rousseau, Bentham, Mill, Dickens, Carlyle, Ruskin, George, Butler, and Morris all rolled into one, with Euripides, More, Moliere, Shakespear, Beaumarchais, Swift, Goethe, Ibsen, Tolstoy, Moses and the prophets all thrown in (as indeed in some sort I actually am, standing as I do on all their shoulders). The problem being to make heroes out of cowards, we paper apostles and artist-magicians have succeeded only in giving cowards all the sensations of heroes whilst they tolerate every abomination, accept every plunder, and submit to every oppression. Christianity, in making a merit of such submission, has marked only that depth in the abyss at which the very sense of shame is lost. The Christian has been like Dickens' doctor in the debtor's prison, who tells the newcomer of its ineffable peace and security: no duns; no tyrannical collectors of rates, taxes, and rent; no importunate hopes nor exacting duties; nothing but the rest and safety of having no further to fall.

Yet in the poorest corner of this soul-destroying Christendom vitality suddenly begins to germinate again. Joyousness, a sacred gift long dethroned by the hellish laughter of derision and obscenity, rises like a flood miraculously out of the fetid dust and mud of the slums; rousing marches and impetuous dithyrambs rise to the heavens from people among whom the depressing noise called "sacred music" is a standing joke; a flag with Blood and Fire on it is unfurled, not in murderous rancor, but because fire is beautiful and blood a vital and splendid red; Fear, which we flatter by calling Self, vanishes; and transfigured men and women carry their gospel through a transfigured world, calling their leader General, themselves captains and brigadiers, and their whole body an Army: praying, but praying only for refreshment, for strength to fight, and for needful MONEY (a notable sign, that); preaching, but not preaching submission; daring ill-usage and abuse, but not putting up with more of it than is inevitable; and practising what the world will let them practise, including soap and water, color and music. There is danger in such Activity; and where there is danger there is hope. Our present security is nothing, and can be nothing, but evil made irresistible.

WEAKNESSES OF THE SALVATION ARMY.

For the present, however, it is not my business to flatter the Salvation Army. Rather must I point out to it that it has almost as many weaknesses as the Church of England itself. It is building up a business organization which will compel it eventually to see that its present staff of enthusiast-commanders shall be succeeded by a bureaucracy of men of business who will be no better than bishops, and perhaps a good deal more unscrupulous. That has always happened sooner or later to great orders founded by saints; and the order founded by St William Booth is not exempt from the same danger. It is even more dependent than the Church on rich people who would cut off supplies at once if it began to preach that indispensable revolt against poverty which must also be a revolt against riches. It is hampered by a heavy contingent of pious elders who are not really Salvationists at all, but Evangelicals of the old school. It still, as Commissioner Howard affirms, "sticks to Moses," which is flat nonsense at this time of day if the Commissioner means, as I am afraid he does, that the Book of Genesis contains a trustworthy scientific account of the origin of species, and that the god to whom Jephthah sacrificed his daughter is any less obviously a tribal idol than Dagon or Chemosh.

Further, there is still too much other-worldliness about the Army. Like Frederick's grenadier, the Salvationist wants to live for ever (the most monstrous way of crying for the moon); and though it is evident to anyone who has ever heard General Booth and his best officers that they would work as hard for human salvation as they do at present if they believed that death would be the end of them individually, they and their followers have a bad habit of talking as if the Salvationists were heroically enduring a very bad time on earth as an investment which will bring them in dividends later on in the form, not of a better life to come for the whole world, but of an eternity spent by themselves personally in a sort of bliss which would bore any active person to a second death. Surely the truth is that the Salvationists are unusually happy people. And is it not the very diagnostic of true salvation that it shall overcome the fear of death? Now the man who has come to believe that there is no such thing as death, the change so called being merely the transition to an exquisitely happy and utterly careless life, has not overcome the fear of death at all: on the contrary, it has overcome him so completely that he refuses to die on any terms whatever. I do not call a Salvationist really saved until he is ready to lie down cheerfully on the scrap heap, having paid scot and lot and something over, and let his eternal life pass on to renew its youth in the battalions of the future.

Then there is the nasty lying habit called confession, which the Army encourages because it lends itself to dramatic oratory, with plenty of thrilling incident. For my part, when I hear a convert relating the violences and oaths and blasphemies he was guilty of before he was saved, making out that he was a very terrible fellow then and is the most contrite and chastened of Christians now, I believe him no more than I believe the millionaire who says he came up to London or Chicago as a boy with only three halfpence in his pocket. Salvationists have said to me that Barbara in my play would never have been taken in by so transparent a humbug as Snobby Price; and certainly I do not think Snobby could have taken in any experienced Salvationist on a point on which the Salvationist did not wish to be taken in. But on the point of conversion all Salvationists wish to be taken in; for the more obvious the sinner the more obvious the miracle of his conversion. When you advertize a converted burglar or reclaimed drunkard as one of the attractions at an experience meeting, your burglar can hardly have been too burglarious or your drunkard too drunken. As long as such attractions are relied on, you will have your Snobbies claiming to have beaten their mothers when they were as a matter of prosaic fact habitually beaten by them, and your Rummies of the tamest respectability pretending to a past of reckless and dazzling vice. Even when confessions are sincerely autobiographic there is no reason to assume at once that the impulse to make them is pious or the interest of the hearers wholesome. It might as well be assumed that the poor people who insist on showing appalling ulcers to district visitors are convinced hygienists, or that the curiosity which sometimes welcomes such exhibitions is a pleasant and creditable one. One is often tempted to suggest that those who pester our police superintendents with confessions of murder might very wisely be taken at their word and executed, except in the few cases in which a real murderer is seeking to be relieved of his guilt by confession and expiation. For though I am not, I hope, an unmerciful person, I do not think that the inexorability of the deed once done should be disguised by any ritual, whether in the confessional or on the scaffold.

And here my disagreement with the Salvation Army, and with all propagandists of the Cross (to which I object as I object to all gibbets) becomes deep indeed. Forgiveness, absolution, atonement, are figments: punishment is only a pretence of cancelling one crime by another; and you can no more have forgiveness without vindictiveness than you can have a cure without a disease. You will never get a high morality from people who conceive that their misdeeds are revocable and pardonable, or in a society where absolution and expiation are officially provided for us all. The demand may be very real; but the supply is spurious. Thus Bill Walker, in my play, having assaulted the Salvation Lass, presently finds himself overwhelmed with an intolerable conviction of sin under the skilled treatment of Barbara. Straightway he begins to try to unassault the lass and deruffianize his deed, first by getting punished for it in kind, and, when that relief is denied him, by fining himself a pound to compensate the girl. He is foiled both ways. He finds the Salvation Army as inexorable as fact itself. It will not punish him: it will not take his money. It will not tolerate a redeemed ruffian: it leaves him no means of salvation except ceasing to be a ruffian. In doing this, the Salvation Army instinctively grasps the central truth of Christianity and discards its central superstition: that central truth being the vanity of revenge and punishment, and that central superstition the salvation of the world by the gibbet.

For, be it noted, Bill has assaulted an old and starving woman also; and for this worse offence he feels no remorse whatever, because she makes it clear that her malice is as great as his own. "Let her have the law of me, as she said she would," says Bill: "what I done to her is no more on what you might call my conscience than sticking a pig." This shows a perfectly natural and wholesome state of mind on his part. The old woman, like the law she threatens him with, is perfectly ready to play the game of retaliation with him: to rob him if he steals, to flog him if he strikes, to murder him if he kills. By example and precept the law and public opinion teach him to impose his will on others by anger, violence, and cruelty, and to wipe off the moral score by punishment. That is sound Crosstianity. But this Crosstianity has got entangled with something which Barbara calls Christianity, and which unexpectedly causes her to refuse to play the hangman's game of Satan casting out Satan. She refuses to prosecute a drunken ruffian; she converses on equal terms with a blackguard whom no lady could be seen speaking to in the public street: in short, she behaves as illegally and unbecomingly as possible under the circumstances. Bill's conscience reacts to this just as naturally as it does to the old woman's threats. He is placed in a position of unbearable moral inferiority, and strives by every means in his power to escape from it, whilst he is still quite ready to meet the abuse of the old woman by attempting to smash a mug on her face. And that is the triumphant justification of Barbara's Christianity as against our system of judicial punishment and the vindictive villain-thrashings and "poetic justice" of the romantic stage.

For the credit of literature it must be pointed out that the situation is only partly novel. Victor Hugo long ago gave us the epic of the convict and the bishop's candlesticks, of the Crosstian policeman annihilated by his encounter with the Christian Valjean. But Bill Walker is not, like Valjean, romantically changed from a demon into an angel. There are millions of Bill Walkers in all classes of society to-day; and the point which I, as a professor of natural psychology, desire to demonstrate, is that Bill, without any change in his character whatsoever, will react one way to one sort of treatment and another way to another.

In proof I might point to the sensational object lesson provided by our commercial millionaires to-day. They begin as brigands: merciless, unscrupulous, dealing out ruin and death and slavery to their competitors and employees, and facing desperately the worst that their competitors can do to them. The history of the English factories, the American trusts, the exploitation of African gold, diamonds, ivory and rubber, outdoes in villainy the worst that has ever been imagined of the buccaneers of the Spanish Main. Captain Kidd would have marooned a modern Trust magnate for conduct unworthy of a gentleman of fortune. The law every day seizes on unsuccessful scoundrels of this type and punishes them with a cruelty worse than their own, with the result that they come out of the torture house more dangerous than they went in, and renew their evil doing (nobody will employ them at anything else) until they are again seized, again tormented, and again let loose, with the same result.

But the successful scoundrel is dealt with very differently, and very Christianly. He is not only forgiven: he is idolized, respected, made much of, all but worshipped. Society returns him good for evil in the most extravagant overmeasure. And with what result? He begins to idolize himself, to respect himself, to live up to the treatment he receives. He preaches sermons; he writes books of the most edifying advice to young men, and actually persuades himself that he got on by taking his own advice; he endows educational institutions; he supports charities; he dies finally in the odor of sanctity, leaving a will which is a monument of public spirit and bounty. And all this without any change in his character. The spots of the leopard and the stripes of the tiger are as brilliant as ever; but the conduct of the world towards him has changed; and his conduct has changed accordingly. You have only to reverse your attitude towards him— to lay hands on his property, revile him, assault him, and he will be a brigand again in a moment, as ready to crush you as you are to crush him, and quite as full of pretentious moral reasons for doing it.

In short, when Major Barbara says that there are no scoundrels, she is right: there are no absolute scoundrels, though there are impracticable people of whom I shall treat presently. Every practicable man (and woman) is a potential scoundrel and a potential good citizen. What a man is depends on his character; but what he does, and what we think of what he does, depends on his circumstances. The characteristics that ruin a man in one class make him eminent in another. The characters that behave differently in different circumstances behave alike in similar circumstances. Take a common English character like that of Bill Walker. We meet Bill everywhere: on the judicial bench, on the episcopal bench, in the Privy

Council, at the War Office and Admiralty, as well as in the Old Bailey dock or in the ranks of casual unskilled labor. And the morality of Bill's characteristics varies with these various circumstances. The faults of the burglar are the qualities of the financier: the manners and habits of a duke would cost a city clerk his situation. In short, though character is independent of circumstances, conduct is not; and our moral judgments of character are not: both are circumstantial. Take any condition of life in which the circumstances are for a mass of men practically alike: felony, the House of Lords, the factory, the stables, the gipsy encampment or where you please! In spite of diversity of character and temperament, the conduct and morals of the individuals in each group are as predicable and as alike in the main as if they were a flock of sheep, morals being mostly only social habits and circumstantial necessities. Strong people know this and count upon it. In nothing have the master-minds of the world been distinguished from the ordinary suburban season-ticket holder more than in their straightforward perception of the fact that mankind is practically a single species, and not a menagerie of gentlemen and bounders, villains and heroes, cowards and daredevils, peers and peasants, grocers and aristocrats, artisans and laborers, washerwomen and duchesses, in which all the grades of income and caste represent distinct animals who must not be introduced to one another or intermarry. Napoleon constructing a galaxy of generals and courtiers, and even of monarchs, out of his collection of social nobodies; Julius Caesar appointing as governor of Egypt the son of a freedman—one who but a short time before would have been legally disqualified for the post even of a private soldier in the Roman army; Louis XI making his barber his privy councillor: all these had in their different ways a firm hold of the scientific fact of human equality, expressed by Barbara in the Christian formula that all men are children of one father. A man who believes that men are naturally divided into upper and lower and middle classes morally is making exactly the same mistake as the man who believes that they are naturally divided in the same way socially. And just as our persistent attempts to found political institutions on a basis of social inequality have always produced long periods of destructive friction relieved from time to time by violent explosions of revolution; so the attempt—will Americans please note—to found moral institutions on a basis of moral inequality can lead to nothing but unnatural Reigns of the Saints relieved by licentious Restorations; to Americans who have made divorce a public institution turning the face of Europe into one huge sardonic smile by refusing to stay in the same hotel with a Russian man of genius who has changed wives without the sanction of South Dakota; to grotesque hypocrisy, cruel persecution, and final utter confusion of conventions and compliances with benevolence and respectability. It is quite useless to declare that all men are born free if you deny that they are born good. Guarantee a man's goodness and his liberty will take care of itself. To guarantee his freedom on condition that you approve of his moral character is formally to abolish all freedom whatsoever, as every man's liberty is at the mercy of a moral indictment, which any fool can trump up against everyone who violates custom, whether as a prophet or as a rascal. This is the lesson Democracy has to learn before it can become anything but the most oppressive of all the priesthoods.

Let us now return to Bill Walker and his case of conscience against the Salvation Army. Major Barbara, not being a modern Tetzel, or the treasurer of a hospital, refuses to sell Bill absolution for a sovereign. Unfortunately, what the Army can afford to refuse in the case of Bill Walker, it cannot refuse in the case of Bodger. Bodger is master of the situation because he holds the purse strings. "Strive as you will," says Bodger, in effect: "me you cannot do without. You cannot save Bill Walker without my money." And the Army answers, quite rightly under the circumstances, "We will take money from the devil himself sooner than abandon the work of Salvation." So Bodger pays his conscience-money and gets the absolution that is refused to Bill. In real life Bill would perhaps never know this. But I, the dramatist, whose business it is to show the connexion between things that seem apart and unrelated in the haphazard order of events in real life, have contrived to make it known to Bill, with the result that the Salvation Army loses its hold of him at once.

But Bill may not be lost, for all that. He is still in the grip of the facts and of his own conscience, and may find his taste for blackguardism permanently spoiled. Still, I cannot guarantee that happy ending. Let anyone walk through the poorer quarters of our cities when the men are not working, but resting and chewing the cud of their reflections; and he will find that there is one expression on every mature face: the expression of cynicism. The discovery made by Bill Walker about the Salvation Army has been made by every one of them. They have found that every man has his price; and they have been foolishly or corruptly taught to mistrust and despise him for that necessary and salutary condition of social existence. When they learn that General Booth, too, has his price, they do not admire him because it is a high one, and admit the need of organizing society so that he shall get it in an honorable way: they conclude that his character is unsound and that all religious men are hypocrites and allies of their sweaters and oppressors. They know that the large subscriptions which help to support the Army are endowments, not of religion, but of the wicked doctrine of docility in poverty and humility under oppression; and they are rent by the most agonizing of all the doubts of the soul, the doubt whether their true salvation must not come from their most abhorrent passions, from murder, envy, greed, stubbornness, rage, and terrorism, rather than from public spirit, reasonableness, humanity, generosity, tenderness, delicacy, pity and kindness. The confirmation of that doubt, at which our newspapers have been working so hard for years past, is the morality of militarism; and the justification of militarism is that circumstances may at any time make it the true morality of the moment. It is by producing such moments that we produce violent and sanguinary revolutions, such as the one now in progress in Russia and the one which Capitalism in England and America is daily and diligently provoking.

At such moments it becomes the duty of the Churches to evoke all the powers of destruction against the existing order. But if they do this, the existing order must forcibly suppress them. Churches are suffered to exist only on condition that they preach submission to the State as at present capitalistically organized. The Church of England itself is compelled to add to the thirty-six articles in which it formulates its religious tenets, three more in which it apologetically protests that the moment any of these articles comes in conflict with the State it is to be entirely renounced, abjured, violated, abrogated and abhorred, the policeman being a much more important person than any of the Persons of the Trinity. And this is why no tolerated Church nor Salvation Army can ever win the entire confidence of the poor. It must be on the side of the police and the military, no matter what it believes or disbelieves; and as the police and the military are the instruments by which the rich rob and oppress the poor (on legal and moral principles made for the purpose), it is not possible to be on the side of the poor and of the police at the same time. Indeed the religious bodies, as the almoners of the rich, become a sort of auxiliary police, taking off the insurrectionary edge of poverty with coals and blankets, bread and treacle, and soothing and cheering the victims with hopes of immense and inexpensive happiness in another world when the process of working them to premature death in the service of the rich is complete in this.

CHRISTIANITY AND ANARCHISM

Such is the false position from which neither the Salvation Army nor the Church of England nor any other religious organization whatever can escape except through a reconstitution of society. Nor can they merely endure the State passively, washing their hands of its sins. The State is constantly forcing the consciences of men by violence and cruelty. Not content with exacting money from us for the maintenance of its soldiers and policemen, its gaolers and executioners, it forces us to take an active personal part in its proceedings on pain of becoming ourselves the victims of its violence. As I write these lines, a sensational example is given to the world. A royal marriage has been celebrated, first by sacrament in a cathedral, and then by a bullfight having for its main amusement the spectacle of horses gored and disembowelled by the bull, after which, when the bull is so exhausted as to be no longer dangerous, he is killed by a cautious matador. But the ironic contrast between the bullfight and the sacrament of marriage does not move anyone. Another contrast—that between the splendor, the happiness, the atmosphere of kindly admiration surrounding the young couple, and the price paid for it under our abominable social arrangements in the misery, squalor and degradation of millions of other young couples—is drawn at the same moment by a novelist, Mr Upton Sinclair, who chips a corner of the veneering from the huge meat packing industries of Chicago, and shows it to us as a sample of what is going on all over the world underneath the top layer of prosperous plutocracy. One man is sufficiently moved by that contrast to pay his own life as the price of one terrible blow at the responsible parties. Unhappily his poverty leaves him also ignorant enough to be duped by the pretence that the innocent young bride and bridegroom, put forth and crowned by plutocracy as the heads of a State in which they have less personal power than any policeman, and less influence than any chairman of a trust, are responsible. At them accordingly he launches his sixpennorth of fulminate, missing his mark, but scattering the bowels of as many horses as any bull in the arena, and slaying twenty-three persons, besides wounding ninety-nine. And of all these, the horses alone are innocent of the guilt he is avenging: had he blown all Madrid to atoms with every adult person in it, not one could have escaped the charge of being an accessory, before, at, and after the fact, to poverty and prostitution, to such wholesale massacre of infants as Herod never dreamt of, to plague, pestilence and famine, battle, murder and lingering death—perhaps not one who had not helped, through example, precept, connivance, and even clamor, to teach the dynamiter his well-learnt gospel of hatred and vengeance, by approving every day of sentences of years of imprisonment so infernal in its unnatural stupidity and panic-stricken cruelty, that their advocates can disavow neither the dagger nor the bomb without stripping the mask of justice and humanity from themselves also. Be it noted that at this very moment there appears the biography of one of our dukes, who, being Scotch, could argue about politics, and therefore stood out as a great brain among our aristocrats. And what, if you please, was his grace's favorite historical episode, which he declared he never read without intense satisfaction? Why, the young General Bonapart's pounding of the Paris mob to pieces in 1795, called in playful approval by our respectable classes "the whiff of grapeshot," though Napoleon, to do him justice, took a deeper view of it, and would fain have had it forgotten. And since the Duke of Argyll was not a demon, but a man of like passions with ourselves, by no means rancorous or cruel as men go, who can doubt that all over the world proletarians of the ducal kidney are now revelling in "the whiff of dynamite" (the flavor of the joke seems to evaporate a little, does it not?) because it was aimed at the class they hate even as our argute duke hated what he called the mob.

In such an atmosphere there can be only one sequel to the Madrid explosion. All Europe burns to emulate it. Vengeance! More blood! Tear "the Anarchist beast" to shreds. Drag him to the scaffold. Imprison him for life. Let all civilized States band together to drive his like off the face of the earth; and if any State refuses to join, make war on it. This time the leading London newspaper, anti-Liberal and therefore anti-Russian in politics, does not say "Serve you right" to the victims, as it did, in effect, when Bobrikofl; and De Plehve, and Grand Duke Sergius, were in the same manner unofficially fulminated into fragments. No: fulminate our rivals in Asia by all means, ye brave Russian revolutionaries; but to aim at an English princess-monstrous! hideous! hound down the wretch to his doom; and observe, please, that we are a civilized and merciful people, and, however much we may regret it, must not treat him as Ravaillac and Damiens were treated. And meanwhile, since we have not yet caught him, let us soothe our quivering nerves with the bullfight, and comment in a courtly way on the unfailing tact and good taste of the ladies of our royal houses, who, though presumably of full normal natural tenderness, have been so effectually broken in to fashionable routine that they can be taken to see the horses slaughtered as helplessly as they could no doubt be taken to a gladiator show, if that happened to be the mode just now.

Strangely enough, in the midst of this raging fire of malice, the one man who still has faith in the kindness and intelligence of human nature is the fulminator, now a hunted wretch, with nothing, apparently, to secure his triumph over all the prisons and scaffolds of infuriate Europe except the revolver in his pocket and his readiness to discharge it at a moment's notice into his own or any other head. Think of him setting out to find a gentleman and a Christian in the multitude of human wolves howling for his blood. Think also of this: that at the very first essay he finds what he seeks, a veritable grandee of Spain, a noble, high-thinking, unterrified, malice-void soul, in the guise—of all masquerades in the world!—of a modern editor. The Anarchist wolf, flying from the wolves of plutocracy, throws himself on the honor of the man. The man, not being a wolf (nor a London editor), and therefore not having enough sympathy with his exploit to be made bloodthirsty by it, does not throw him back to the pursuing wolves—gives him, instead, what help he can to escape, and sends him off acquainted at last with a force that goes deeper than dynamite, though you cannot make so much of it for sixpence. That righteous and honorable high human deed is not wasted on Europe, let us hope, though it benefits the fugitive wolf only for a moment. The plutocratic wolves presently smell him out. The fugitive shoots the unlucky wolf whose nose is nearest; shoots himself; and then convinces the world, by his photograph, that he was no monstrous freak of reversion to the tiger, but a good looking young man with nothing abnormal about him except his appalling courage and resolution (that is why the terrified shriek Coward at him): one to whom murdering a happy young couple on their wedding morning would have been an unthinkably unnatural abomination under rational and kindly human circumstances.

Then comes the climax of irony and blind stupidity. The wolves, balked of their meal of fellow-wolf, turn on the man, and proceed to torture him, after their manner, by imprisonment, for refusing to fasten his teeth in the throat of the dynamiter and hold him down until they came to finish him.

Thus, you see, a man may not be a gentleman nowadays even if he wishes to. As to being a Christian, he is allowed some latitude in that matter, because, I repeat, Christianity has two faces. Popular Christianity has for its emblem a gibbet, for its chief sensation a sanguinary execution after torture, for its central mystery an insane vengeance bought off by a trumpery expiation. But there is a nobler and profounder Christianity which affirms the sacred mystery of Equality, and forbids the glaring futility and folly of vengeance, often politely called punishment or justice. The gibbet part of Christianity is tolerated. The other is criminal felony. Connoisseurs in irony are well aware of the fact that the only editor in England who denounces punishment as radically wrong, also repudiates Christianity; calls his paper The Freethinker; and has been imprisoned for two years for blasphemy.

SANE CONCLUSIONS

And now I must ask the excited reader not to lose his head on one side or the other, but to draw a sane moral from these grim absurdities. It is not good sense to propose that laws against crime should apply to principals only and not to accessories whose consent, counsel, or silence may secure impunity to the principal. If you institute punishment as part of the law, you must punish people for refusing to punish. If you have a police, part of its duty must be to compel everybody to assist the police. No doubt if your laws are unjust, and your policemen agents of oppression, the result will be an unbearable violation of the private consciences of citizens. But that cannot be helped: the remedy is, not to license everybody to thwart the law if they please, but to make laws that will command the public assent, and not to deal cruelly and stupidly with lawbreakers. Everybody disapproves of burglars; but the modern burglar, when caught and overpowered by a householder usually appeals, and often, let us hope, with success, to his captor not to deliver him over to the useless horrors of penal servitude. In other cases the lawbreaker escapes because those who could give him up do not consider his breech of the law a guilty action. Sometimes, even, private tribunals are formed in opposition to the official tribunals; and these private tribunals employ assassins as executioners, as was done, for example, by Mahomet before he had established his power officially, and by the Ribbon lodges of Ireland in their long struggle with the landlords. Under such circumstances, the assassin goes free although everybody in the district knows who he is and what he has done. They do not betray him, partly because they justify him exactly as the regular Government justifies its official executioner, and partly because they would themselves be assassinated if they betrayed him: another method learnt from the official government. Given a tribunal, employing a slayer who has no personal quarrel with the slain; and there is clearly no moral difference between official and unofficial killing.

In short, all men are anarchists with regard to laws which are against their consciences, either in the preamble or in the penalty. In London our worst anarchists are the magistrates, because many of them are so old and ignorant that when they are called upon to administer any law that is based on ideas or knowledge less than half a century old, they disagree with it, and being mere ordinary homebred private Englishmen without any respect for law in the abstract, naively set the example of violating it. In this instance the man lags behind the law; but when the law lags behind the man, he becomes equally an anarchist. When some huge change in social conditions, such as the industrial revolution of the eighteenth and nineteenth centuries, throws our legal and industrial institutions out of date, Anarchism becomes almost a religion. The whole force of the most energetic geniuses of the time in philosophy, economics, and art, concentrates itself on demonstrations and reminders that morality and law are only conventions, fallible and continually obsolescing. Tragedies in which the heroes are bandits, and comedies in which law-abiding and conventionally moral folk are compelled to satirize themselves by outraging the conscience of the spectators every time they do their duty, appear simultaneously with economic treatises entitled "What is Property? Theft!" and with histories of "The Conflict between Religion and Science."

Now this is not a healthy state of things. The advantages of living in society are proportionate, not to the freedom of the individual from a code, but to the complexity and subtlety of the code he is prepared not only to accept but to uphold as a matter of such vital importance that a lawbreaker at large is hardly to be tolerated on any plea. Such an attitude becomes impossible when the only men who can make themselves heard and remembered throughout the world spend all their energy in raising our gorge against current law, current morality, current respect ability, and legal property. The ordinary man, uneducated in social theory even when he is schooled in Latin verse, cannot be set against all the laws of his country and yet persuaded to regard law in the abstract as vitally necessary to society. Once he is brought to repudiate the laws and institutions he knows, he will repudiate the very conception of law and the very groundwork of institutions, ridiculing human rights, extolling brainless methods as "historical," and tolerating nothing except pure empiricism in conduct, with dynamite as the basis of politics and vivisection as the basis of science. That is hideous; but what is to be done? Here am I, for instance, by class a respectable man, by common sense a hater of waste and disorder, by intellectual constitution legally minded to the verge of pedantry, and by temperament apprehensive and economically disposed to the limit of old-maidishness; yet I am, and have always been, and shall now always be, a revolutionary writer, because our laws make law impossible; our liberties destroy all freedom; our property is organized robbery; our morality is an impudent hypocrisy; our wisdom is administered by inexperienced or malexperienced dupes, our power wielded by cowards and weaklings, and our honor false in all its points. I am an enemy of the existing order for good reasons; but that does not make my attacks any less encouraging or helpful to people who are its enemies for bad reasons. The existing order may shriek that if I tell the truth about it, some foolish person may drive it to become still worse by trying to assassinate it. I cannot help that, even if I could see what worse it could do than it is already doing. And the disadvantage of that worst even from its own point of view is that society, with all its prisons and bayonets and whips and ostracisms and starvations, is powerless in the face of the Anarchist who is prepared to sacrifice his own life in the battle with it. Our natural safety from the cheap and devastating explosives which every Russian student can make, and every Russian grenadier has learnt to handle in Manchuria, lies in the fact that brave and resolute men, when they are rascals, will not risk their skins for the good of humanity, and, when they are sympathetic enough to care for humanity, abhor murder, and never commit it until their consciences are outraged beyond endurance. The remedy is, simply not to outrage their consciences.

Do not be afraid that they will not make allowances. All men make very large allowances indeed before they stake their own lives in a war to the death with society. Nobody demands or expects the millennium. But there are two things that must be set right, or we shall perish, like Rome, of soul atrophy disguised as empire. The first is, that the daily ceremony of dividing the wealth of the country among its inhabitants shall be so conducted that no crumb shall go to any able-bodied adults who are not producing by their personal exertions not only a full equivalent for what they take, but a surplus sufficient to provide for their superannuation and pay back the debt due for their nurture.

The second is that the deliberate infliction of malicious injuries which now goes on under the name of punishment be abandoned; so that the thief, the ruffian, the gambler, and the beggar, may without inhumanity be handed over to the law, and made to understand that a State which is too humane to punish will also be too thrifty to waste the life of honest men in watching or restraining dishonest ones. That is why we do not imprison dogs. We even take our chance of their first bite. But if a dog delights to bark and bite, it goes to the lethal chamber. That seems to me sensible. To allow the dog to expiate his bite by a period of torment, and then let him loose in a much more savage condition (for the chain makes a dog savage) to bite again and expiate again, having meanwhile spent a great deal of human life and happiness in the task of chaining and feeding and tormenting him, seems to me idiotic and superstitious. Yet that is what we do to men who bark and bite and steal. It would be far more sensible to put up with their vices, as we put up with their illnesses, until they give more trouble than they are worth, at which point we should, with many apologies and expressions of sympathy, and some generosity in complying with their last wishes, then, place them in the lethal chamber and get rid of them. Under no circumstances should they be allowed to expiate their misdeeds by a manufactured penalty, to subscribe to a charity, or to compensate the victims. If there is to be no punishment there can be no forgiveness. We shall never have real moral responsibility until everyone knows that his deeds are irrevocable, and that his life depends on his usefulness. Hitherto, alas! humanity has never dared face these hard facts. We frantically scatter conscience money and invent systems of conscience banking, with expiatory penalties, atonements, redemptions, salvations, hospital subscription lists and what not, to enable us to contract-out of the moral code. Not content with the old scapegoat and sacrificial lamb, we deify human saviors, and pray to miraculous virgin intercessors. We attribute mercy to the inexorable; soothe our consciences after committing murder by throwing ourselves on the bosom of divine love; and shrink even from our own gallows because we are forced to admit that it, at least, is irrevocable—as if one hour of imprisonment were not as irrevocable as any execution!

If a man cannot look evil in the face without illusion, he will never know what it really is, or combat it effectually. The few men who have been able (relatively) to do this have been called cynics, and have sometimes had an abnormal share of evil in themselves, corresponding to the abnormal strength of their minds; but they have never done mischief unless they intended to do it. That is why great scoundrels have been beneficent rulers whilst amiable and privately harmless monarchs have ruined their countries by trusting to the hocus-pocus of innocence and guilt, reward and punishment, virtuous indignation and pardon, instead of standing up to the facts without either malice or mercy. Major Barbara stands up to Bill Walker in that way, with the result that the ruffian who cannot get hated, has to hate himself. To relieve this agony he tries to get punished; but the Salvationist whom he tries to provoke is as merciless as Barbara, and only prays for him. Then he tries to pay, but can get nobody to take his money. His doom is the doom of Cain, who, failing to find either a savior, a policeman, or an almoner to help him to pretend that his brother's blood no longer cried from the ground, had to live and die a murderer. Cain took care not to commit another murder, unlike our railway shareholders (I am one) who kill and maim shunters by hundreds to save the cost of automatic couplings, and make atonement by annual subscriptions to deserving charities. Had Cain been allowed to pay off his score, he might possibly have killed Adam and Eve for the mere sake of a second luxurious reconciliation with God afterwards. Bodger, you may depend on it, will go on to the end of his life poisoning people with bad whisky, because he can always depend on the Salvation Army or the Church of England to negotiate a redemption for him in consideration of a trifling percentage of his profits. There is a third condition too, which must be fulfilled before the great teachers of the world will cease to scoff at its religions. Creeds must become intellectually honest. At present there is not a single credible established religion in the world. That is perhaps the most stupendous fact in the whole world-situation. This play of mine, Major Barbara, is, I hope, both true and inspired; but whoever says that it all happened, and that faith in it and understanding of it consist in believing that it is a record of an actual occurrence, is, to speak according to Scripture, a fool and a liar, and is hereby solemnly denounced and cursed as such by me, the author, to all posterity.

London, June 1906.